This book belongs to

....

Jade

The Clockwork City

Jade

The Clockwork City

Rose Lacey

Willow
Tree

A CIP catalogue record for this book is
available from the British Library

Published by Willow Tree Books, 2018
Willow Tree Books, Tide Mill Way, Woodbridge, Suffolk, IP12 1AP

0 2 4 6 8 9 7 5 3 1

Series concept © 2018 Willow Tree Books
Text © 2018 Working Partners Limited
London, WC1X 9HH
Cover illustration © 2018 Willow Tree Books
Interior illustrations © 2018 Willow Tree Books

Special thanks to Lil Chase

Willow Tree Books, Princess Pirates and associated logos are
trademarks and/or registered trademarks of Imagine That Group Ltd

ISBN: 978-1-78700-448-1
Printed and bound in Great Britain
by Bell and Bain Ltd, Glasgow

www.willowtreebooks.net

**To Eloise Tarlowski,
and her gem of a mother**

Prologue

It has been ten years since the battle that changed everything. Ten long years since the kingdoms fell. And I – Celestine the seawitch – have been trying to reunite the five princesses ever since.

When evil Obsidian defeated the kings and queens of Lemuria, I stood on the burning ship with them as cannon fire rained down all around us. We all knew Obsidian had won. Despite my powers, I couldn't save the kings and queens, but I could make sure I saved their children. I placed the five baby girls in baskets, with the magical rings of their home islands, and cast them out to sea. All in the hope that one day they would return, use the 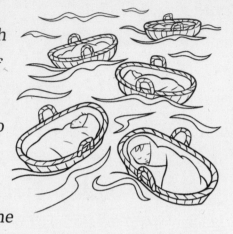 rings to find the magical Treasures, claim their thrones, and fulfil their destinies.

I found Topaz, Pearl, Coral and Opal when they were still just infants or toddlers. But Jade had vanished.

Until now.

At last, ten years since that terrible battle, I have found Jade in a foster home. She seems well cared for and as healthy and happy as any normal ten-year-old. I look out into the garden and see her making something. She twists and fiddles

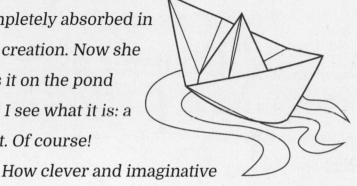

with it in her hands, completely absorbed in her creation. Now she sets it on the pond and I see what it is: a boat. Of course!

How clever and imaginative Jade is. She'll need those talents when she gets back to Lemuria. She'll need them to fight the wicked Obsidian.

For a moment, I am tempted to turn around and leave Jade here, in this safe place. She knows nothing of the challenges ahead. But I know I must take her. I will keep her close and watch over her, as I have done the other princesses.

For one day they will return to their world. And they will take it back ...

Chapter 1

The roar of the crowd was almost deafening and Jade was swept up in the excitement. It was the school's sports day and the students at Breakwater Hall were down by the huge lake, whooping and waving flags as eight fellow pupils swam the 200-metre race in the cool, clear water. Jade had only been at Breakwater Hall for a few weeks but she'd made lots of friends. Still, there was only one person she rooted for now.

"Come on, Pearl!" she yelled.

Pearl was one of her four dorm mates, one of

her best friends ... and the bounciest person she'd ever met! Pearl's arms windmilled as she front-crawled towards the finish line. She was the youngest and smallest person in the race, but she was in second place and gradually catching up with the leader.

"You can do it, Pearl!" cried Coral, standing next to Jade.

But the older girl passed the finish line first, Pearl just a fingertip behind.

"Second place," Jade cheered. "That's amazing!"

"That's our girl, Pearl!" whooped Topaz.

"We knew you could do it!" shouted Opal.

Pearl bounded out of the water and ran straight towards them, not even stopping to grab a towel. Her blonde pigtails were dripping and her cheeks were rosy. "Did you see me? Did you see me?"

"We did!" Jade told her. "Second place against all those older girls! Let me give you a hug."

"But I'm all wet," said Pearl.

"What's a few drops of water between friends?" said Jade, squeezing her tightly.

The three other girls piled in for a big group hug. The five friends were the only orphans at the school, which meant they lived at Breakwater Hall all year round. But more than that, they shared a secret that meant their bond was stronger than anything.

Pearl giggled. "It would have been first place if I'd had my tail," she whispered from the middle of the hug.

Jade grinned as she let Pearl go and looked around. "Shh," she said, "someone might hear you."

Because this was the secret they shared: here, at Breakwater Hall, the five girls were orphans, with no home, family or heirlooms apart from the ring each girl was found with. But some magic those rings contained whisked them away to a secret world where they were princesses! Princess Pirates, no less!

Not only that, but they each had magical powers. Topaz had super-strength, Opal could talk to animals, Coral could control the elements, Pearl could transform into a mermaid ... and Jade was a genius inventor.

She had always been good with machinery and making things, but in Lemuria it was something different – she saw blueprint designs in her head that showed her how to create almost anything! The friends were all desperate to travel back to Lemuria, to find out more about where they came from, and to test out their powers again.

The only trouble was, they had no idea how to get there. Jade looked down at her ring – an oval-shaped green stone set into a gold band. She was sure their rings were the key to returning to Lemuria ... but nothing they'd tried, even ring bumps, had worked.

As they broke apart from the hug, Opal shook her head, her dark hair swishing. "I'm worried," she said, biting her lip. "Lemuria is still in danger with that witch Obsidian roaming around."

"And what about Jasper?" added Jade. Jasper was a friend they'd made in Lemuria. "Who knows what trouble he's wound up in?"

Jade could feel the worry hanging over them like a thundercloud. Topaz sighed and pushed

back her thick locks of auburn hair to look at her schedule of the sports day activities. "What's next? Are you in any swimming races, Jade?"

Jade shook her head rapidly. "I'm supposed to be helping out on the refreshments stall."

"Again?" asked Coral, scrunching up her freckly face. "You've been there all morning."

"I like to help out," Jade smiled, hoping it didn't seem too fake. She had a secret of her own, a secret she hadn't dared to share with her new friends. All four girls had been so kind to her since she arrived, but would they still accept her if they knew?

"Actually—" she started to say.

But just then Miss Whitestone beckoned Jade over from the stall. "Hurry, Jade," she called out. "The swimmers are thirsty!"

Jade couldn't help feeling relieved. She knew she would have to tell her friends the secret eventually ... but not today.

When Jade got to the makeshift stall – a trestle table with a paper tablecloth, set up on the bank of the lake – Miss Whitestone greeted her with a crinkly-eyed smile. "Thanks so much for all your help today, Jade," she said.

Miss Whitestone was Jade's favourite headteacher. And since she'd had no fewer than ten, that was saying something! When Jade was younger, she'd lived in a number of foster homes around the country.

All very nice, but none felt like home. It seemed like fate when Miss Whitestone showed up and offered her a scholarship at Breakwater Hall. Without her she would never have met Topaz, Coral, Pearl and Opal. She'd moved around so

much she'd never had such good friends before. And without her friends, she'd never have found out the truth about her past.

Together, Jade and Miss Whitestone filled plastic beakers with orange squash and set out plates of cakes and biscuits for the hungry competitors. The food and drink disappeared into grateful hands faster than they could replace it.

The sudden screeching of a megaphone almost made Jade spill a jug of orange squash. "Would the groups taking part in the dorm room challenge get to their boats," announced Mr Sykes, the PE teacher. "The sailing event is about to begin."

Jade felt her stomach drop as she saw her friends running towards her, excitedly.

"Let's go!" cried Pearl.

"Are you coming?" asked Opal, grinning.

"This *is* the dorm room challenge ... and last time

I checked, you're in our dorm."

"Erm ..." Jade's head was spinning.

"And you're our friend," said Coral. "We won't do it without you."

"It's all friends on deck, remember?" added Topaz.

That was the motto the girls had taught Jade on her first day at Breakwater Hall. The motto that had saved Jade's life. She couldn't say no, despite the fear she felt. Because this was her secret: Jade was terrified of water!

What kind of princess pirate is scared of water? she asked herself.

"What's up?" Pearl asked, tilting her head to the side.

Jade forced a smile for about the tenth time that day, and hoped her face wasn't as green as the ring on her finger. "Nothing," she

said. "Let's go."

There were lots of similar boats to choose from at the dock, but everyone at school knew that the five friends only ever sailed in Nestor – the boat with a horse's head painted on to its hull. As they jumped aboard Jade realised she was holding her breath. She watched as her friends took their places, unfurled the sails and started preparing the ropes as calmly as if they were tidying their room, not heading out on to a deep lake.

Coral tucked her thick red hair behind her ears. "That's a pretty tune," she said. "What is it?"

Jade hadn't even realised she'd been humming. "To be honest, I don't know. It's a tune I've had in my head for as long as I can remember. I guess it relaxes me."

"Well, let's hope it brings us luck," said Pearl.

"Ha!" said Topaz, with a grin. "We don't need

luck! We're princess pirates!"

Jade told herself she'd be fine with the other girls around her. Before long they were at the starting line, and Miss Whitestone was sounding the horn to start the race. Topaz was captain as

Jade

The Clockwork City

always; she called out instructions to pull ropes, raise and tighten the sails, always working to make the most of her team, and the wind.

"I wish I had my powers," said Coral. "Then I'd make the wind even stronger, but just for us."

"I think that might be cheating," Opal laughed.

Coral raised an eyebrow. "Where does it say that in the rule book?"

The boat picked up speed and soon they were way out in front, rounding a buoy to head to the small island in the middle of the lake, where the flag they needed to win the race was hidden. Jade shut her eyes in terror as the dinghy lurched to one side before righting itself again. When she opened them again she focused on her ring to calm herself.

Her ring! It was glowing!

"Girls!" she cried. "Look!"

Four mouths dropped open in surprise when they saw the glowing green stone in Jade's ring. Then they all looked at their own rings – they were glowing too!

'Whoa!" gasped Coral.

"Does this mean what I think it means?"

said Pearl, squirming in her seat.

"Only one way to find out," said Topaz. "Come on girls, ring bump!"

"All friends on deck!" the five friends chorused together.

Jade felt a wave of excitement, bigger than any of the ripples on the lake, as the five friends brought their fists forward and touched the stones on their rings together.

A blinding flash of golden light made Jade wince.

When she opened her eyes again she saw

hard wooden planks beneath her, three tall masts above her, and a pink flag with a heart and crossbones fluttering in the salty breeze.

They were back on their pirate ship.

Back in Lemuria at last.

Chapter 2

Jade looked down and smiled. She was wearing leggings tucked into green boots, a yellow shirt, a green jacket and a green tricorn hat with a bow. Her long black plait was tied with another bow. She'd forgotten how much she loved her princess pirate outfit!

Coral clearly felt the same because she was leaning over a barrel of water trying to get a glimpse of her reflection. Pearl jumped up and down with glee, her blonde pigtails bobbing as she did so. "We're back!" she cried, happily.

Opal looked thoughtful. "Do you think our rings glow when Lemuria needs us?" she asked.

Topaz frowned. "I was wondering the same thing," she replied, swishing the cutlass she found in their last adventure through the air.

Jade looked out at the vast ocean that surrounded them and felt relieved that the day was bright and clear and the ocean was calm. Best of all, there was no sign of Obsidian's pirate ship anywhere. Jade wasn't thrilled to be on the water, but it was worth it to be back in Lemuria. The land she was born in.

Topaz started walking towards the back of the ship, where the ship's wheel was. She was the captain of their dinghy and the captain of their pirate ship too. "The ship looks OK," said Topaz, "so let's set sail to check on the Orange Isle."

The Orange Isle was the island where Topaz's family came from. Jade could understand

Topaz's logic, but she desperately wanted to visit her own island, too. Since their last visit they'd all guessed which island was theirs. The Green Isle had to be Jade's: green was her favourite colour ... and jade was a green stone, after all!

"I don't know, Topaz," shrugged Opal. "Maybe we should check on one of the other islands first. Like maybe the Purple Isle?"

"I think we should go to my island," said Pearl, pulling one pigtail. "I'm the youngest."

"Well my name comes first in the alphabet!" Coral offered.

It seemed everyone wanted to visit their own island just as much as Jade did: there was only one fair thing to do.

"Let's draw straws," Jade suggested, but the other girls were all too busy arguing to hear her.

"Ahem!" came a loud cough from the front of

the ship.

"Nestor!" they all cried together, and raced to the foredeck. Nestor was the horse-shaped figurehead at the front of the ship. And he could talk!

"Forgotten about me already, have you?" he said, snorting indignantly.

Opal leaned over the side to stroke his neck. "We could never forget you."

Nestor rocked from side to side. "Are you all ... erm ... shipshape?" asked Jade. "No leaks or anything?"

"Well, there's something tickling my hull

that's rather annoying," Nestor replied. "Fish it out for me, would you?"

The girls jumped into action at once. There, on the starboard side of the ship, was a glass bottle bumping up against Nestor's hull. It glowed with a faint light.

Jade pushed back her fear of the ocean and started thinking about how to get the bottle. She closed her eyes and, just like the last time she was in Lemuria, a blueprint appeared in her mind. She'd need four metres of rope, a metre-long stick and a winch.

"I've got this," she told the others, grabbing a

rope that lay coiled on the deck. "Just give me a second to—"

But Pearl had already jumped into the water. She held the bottle in one hand and waved her purple-green mermaid tail at the girls. "I've been dying to do that for weeks!" she said, grinning up at them.

Jade tied one end of the rope to the railings and threw the other end over the side. The four friends watched in amazement as Pearl's tail transformed back into legs, complete with blue-

and-white striped trousers, as she began to climb the rope. Pearl passed the bottle to Jade as she clambered on to the ship's deck.

Jade looked at the bottle closcly. Its glow faded and spluttered like a candle running out of wax. A scroll of white paper was rolled up inside, and a word was engraved on to the outside of  the glass. "Nestor," she read out loud. "Nestor, the bottle has your name on!"

"Must be how it found me," Nestor replied. "It's been bumping up against my hull for hours. Most uncomfortable."

The girls gathered around Jade as she pulled out the scroll and unrolled it.

"The map!" Jade said with a gasp.

It was the same map they had used on their

last adventure. Drawn on it was the whole of Lemuria, with the five islands where the girls' families had reigned and the smaller island in the centre. Most importantly, it showed where the magical Treasures that had the power to protect Lemuria were hidden. Jasper's parents had made the map, and he'd almost died trying to protect it.

"But if the map is here," said Opal, biting her lip, "where's Jasper?"

A second, smaller piece of paper fell out of the bottle and floated to the floor. Pearl bent down to pick it up.

"It's a note," she said. Then she gasped. "Oh my goodness, it's from Jasper!"

Jade's stomach flipped over with worry. "What does it say?" she asked Pearl.

"Help me!" Pearl read aloud. "I'm being held captive by Obsidian on the Green Isle."

The Green Isle! Jade's stomach flipped again.

That's my island! They'd all seen what Obsidian had done to the Orange Isle, and Jade couldn't bear the idea that the same thing might have happened to the Green Isle and the people who lived there.

"I've been spying on Obsidian," Pearl continued reading, "and she's close to finding the Treasure ... even without this map! You must come quickly!"

"There's no time to lose!" said Jade.

Topaz stood tall. "Opal, get to the main mast, Pearl to the foremast, Coral to the mizzen mast. I'll take the helm and set a course for the Green Isle. Jade, get to the telescope

on the foredeck. First sight of land, you yell!"
Topaz sounded like a real ship's captain. As they
scurried to their positions she shouted more
instructions. "Raise the sails! Full speed ahead!"

Even Nestor joined in when they replied, "Aye
aye, Captain!"

The wind caught the sails and the old boat
leaned into the water as it began to cut through
the waves. They were on their way.

***

Jade didn't take her eye off the telescope for a
moment of their voyage. Finally, she thought she
could make out a shape in the far, far distance.

"Land ahoy!" she shouted, trying to sound
like a pirate and not a schoolgirl who was scared
of water. "I think ..."

Coral climbed the rigging and clambered
into the crow's nest. "Oh, wow, you're right!" she
called down. "You have to see this, Jade."

The mast was higher than the ceiling of the school hall, but while water terrified Jade, heights were no problem. She scrambled quickly up the knotted ropes of the rigging until she reached the crow's nest.

"Take a look at this," said Coral, handing Jade a pocket telescope.

What Jade saw made her suck in a huge breath – rising out of the ocean was a beautiful island, shimmering in the sunlight. She had imagined that the Green Isle would be covered in plants, but in fact the island appeared to be mostly made of metal and ever-so-faintly *glowing* green! As they drew closer, Jade saw cogs, wheels, platforms and levers. In the centre of the island was a large tower, like a mobile phone mast, reaching up into the sky above.

"A clockwork city," Jade breathed.

"This island is *so* you," Coral replied,

squeezing her tight. "You're going home!"

A few minutes later, they pulled into the harbour. The boats at the dock were held in place by strange-looking robot arms. Jade smiled with relief – those arms would keep the ship steady. She would be back on land soon! As Nestor approached, two arms reached out towards them. The arms creaked and groaned as they pulled Nestor into the metal dock wall and held him securely in place.

"I'm not sure about all this modern technology!" Nestor said, tossing his mane grumpily.

"Even without the Treasure," Jade said, "my island seems OK." She sighed with relief.

"Err, yeah," said Topaz. "Except ... where is everyone?"

Jade frowned. Topaz was right – the harbour was completely deserted! She began to feel

sick with worry. "Has Obsidian got rid of all the people?" Jade wondered aloud. "Are we too late?"

There were shops along the seafront, but all of the shutters were closed. Machines dotted the streets but Jade could see that they were covered in brown rust, and many of them looked broken. *My island isn't OK,* thought Jade. *It isn't OK at all.*

"Come on," called Topaz. "Let's go and have a look around."

The girls said goodbye to Nestor and jumped off the boat. They ran through the streets ... but they were all the same – empty and quiet. Jade's feeling of dread grew deeper.

Opal was leading the way. She looked down at the map. "There's a main square over there!" she said. "It should be right around this corner ..."

Jade turned the corner just after Opal. There it was – the large central square of the island,

crowded with people. *So this is where they all are!* But the people were all strangely silent. The clock over the square was broken, one hand hanging off by a thin spring.

"Maybe it's some kind of festival," suggested Coral, as she caught up with the rest of the girls.

The people at the back of the crowd glared at them. A man put his finger to his lips. Their faces looked drawn and tired. Their clothes – boiler suits smeared with grease marks – were torn.

Coral winced. "Not a festival, then," she whispered.

Another woman stared hard at each of the five girls in turn, as if she was counting them. Was she wondering if they were the five princesses? Maybe she could help them find Jasper.

"Excuse me," Jade said, approaching the woman. "But we're—"

"People of the Green Isle!" a loud voice suddenly boomed.

Jade shuddered and looked towards the front of the square. It was Obsidian! She stood on a podium, her dark blue hair scraped back into a tight bun. Her golden crown was fixed on her head like it was stuck with glue and she carried her golden staff, with its glinting black stone at the end.

Obsidian glared down at the people of the Green Isle and Jade knew that they all felt the same dread she did. What was the wicked woman planning?

Chapter 3

Jade gritted her teeth as anger boiled up inside her.

"That witch!" hissed Topaz.

"We ought to go up there right now—" said Coral.

"Shh!" whispered the man in front of them.

Jade got on her tiptoes to see. Obsidian was the reason she was an orphan, the reason all five of them were orphans. She had killed the heads of the royal families of Lemuria so she could become queen of the whole realm.

But the girls' parents had been too smart for her. They had hidden the five Treasures that she would need to rule the islands. But without the Treasures, the islands were dying. The girls had to find the Treasures to bring their islands back to life, and then hide them back at Breakwater Hall, safe from Obsidian.

Beside Obsidian stood her two henchmen: tall, skinny Larry and short, fat Boil. Larry and Boil held their wolves, Snarl and Menace, on leashes. The wolves snapped and growled menacingly.

Obsidian cracked a cruel smile. "You will obey me in everything from now on," she announced to the people below.

Jade clenched her fists. "Who does she think she is?"

Pearl was so short she had to jump up and down to try to see. "There's something weird

about this crowd," she said.

Pearl was right, but Jade couldn't put her finger on what it was.

"Obey me," Obsidian cried, "or your children will die!"

Jade gasped. Suddenly she realised what was so strange. There wasn't one child, one baby, or one teenager among the crowd. Obsidian must have kidnapped them!

The grown-ups started to cry out in distress.

Jade felt desperately sorry for them.

"Please!" a woman shouted from the crowd. "We'll do anything!"

Larry passed Obsidian a large piece of paper. The girls were standing quite far from the podium, but when Obsidian unfurled the paper, Jade recognised the five faces on it: one of them was her own! Above the pictures of the girls was written: WANTED! DEAD OR ALIVE.

"These are the precious princesses of Lemuria," Obsidian spat through her teeth. "But tell me: what's more important to you – these princesses … or your own children?"

"That's it!" Jade growled. She snatched Topaz's cutlass from her side. "I'm going up there right now."

A few people turned to look at her. Like the woman had done before, they counted the girls, then looked at their hands, searching for the

rings. Several of them gasped as they realised who the girls must be.

Before Jade could make her way through the crowd, Topaz grabbed her by the elbow. Since they were on Lemuria, Topaz could use her special power of super-strength. Her grip was so strong that there was no way Jade could move.

"Errrr," said Opal. "I think we'd better go."

Jade saw the desperation of the people around her. They'd do anything to save their children – even turn in the princesses who'd come to help.

Jade and the other girls backed away from the crowd. More and more people turned to look at them.

"We'll save your children," Jade told them. "I promise."

"But right now," said Pearl, "we're off!"

The girls ran as fast as they could, racing past

shops and homes, all of them rusted and run-down. But the next turning led them down an alleyway. The far end was blocked off by a high wall. There was no way out!

Opal's hands shook as she fumbled with the map. "We need to go that way ..." she pointed back towards the main street. "Uh-oh ..."

Jade turned to see what Opal was looking at.

The entrance to the alleyway was now blocked by two shadowy figures.

"Uh-oh is an understatement," whispered Topaz.

Jade swallowed hard. The two people didn't have leashed wolves with them – they weren't Larry and Boil, at least. But right now, since Obsidian had captured the children of the Green Isle, everyone was a potential enemy. She was sure the islanders would hand them over to Obsidian if it meant getting their children back –

and who could blame them?

"I could try calling up a thunderstorm?" Coral suggested.

But the couple raised their hands. They stepped forward and Jade could see a man and a woman, both with the same dark hair and oval eyes, both wearing ragged boiler suits. The woman looked from side to side down the main street before she stepped closer again.

"We know who you are," she whispered softly. "We're not going to hurt you."

Half a smile crept on to the man's face. "You're Lemuria's only hope."

Jade smiled. "We'll do whatever we can," she said. "I'm Jade. I'm—"

The woman rushed forwards, arms outstretched as if to hug her. "Princess Jade, of course!" But then she stopped herself and curtsied. "You look so much like your mother."

Jade's breath caught in her throat.

"She was so beautiful," the woman continued. "Her green eyes ..."

The man bowed. "Princess Jade," he said. "Princess Opal, Princess Topaz, Princess Coral, and Princess Pearl, I presume? It is our honour."

"Thanks very much!" giggled Pearl.

"Can you help us?" Topaz asked.

"Of course," said the man. "We'll hide you

safely in my workshop. I'm Tim and this is my
wife, Tammy."

The couple checked that the main street was
still empty, and beckoned the girls out of the
alleyway. They crept alongside a deserted railway

station. A steam train stood rusting just off the
platform. A big sign outside read "Station closed".

"What happened here?" Jade asked Tammy.

"Oh it's just been awful," Tammy replied,
her hand on her heart. "Your parents hid the

Treasure before they were ..." She gave Jade a sad look. "It was the right thing to do. But ever since, the whole island has been suffering. The steam trains won't go, the walkways are all stuck. The island used to run like clockwork, but now ..." She swept her hand out in front of her to show Jade the ruin that surrounded them. "This thick rust is covering everything. We've tried to paint the metal, tried everything to stop it, but it keeps creeping over the island."

"We've never seen rust like it," Tim chipped in. "It's probably magical."

"But oh, Jade!" Tammy continued. "You should have seen the island in its heyday! People would come to visit our wonderful inventions. The playgrounds, the factories that ran on steam, the machines that did everything we needed."

Coral listened wide-eyed. "Whoa," she said. "Imagine a world where I only had to lift a finger

to get my nails painted."

The girls followed the couple past gigantic greenhouses. Jade pressed her face to the glass and saw that they were filled with brown, wilting plants. There were massive fans attached to the ceilings, but they weren't moving.

"The glass domes and vertical gardens where we have always grown our fresh food are broken," Tim told her. "The plants have died. All we have to eat now is fish and seaweed."

Coral stuck out her tongue in disgust.

"But I would go a lifetime without fresh food if we could just get our children back," Tim sniffed. "When Obsidian took our daughter, my heart broke."

The girls exchanged sympathetic looks as they walked in silence. Eventually, Tammy stopped at a small, rust-covered house, with what looked like a large metal shed next door. "This is

our workshop," she said, opening the door and holding it open for the girls.

Inside was a room with a counter, like the front of a small shop. Behind the counter was a large workshop with machinery piled up all over the floor and hanging from hoists in the ceiling. A metal workbench ran the full length of one side of the room. Hundreds of tools – some that Jade didn't even know the name of – hung on the wall behind it. Jade spun around to take everything in. "This place is my idea of heaven," she breathed.

The rest of the girls chuckled.

"I bet you could make anything out of all this," said Coral.

Jade noticed a teddy bear sitting up on a high shelf. It was well worn, with patchy fur and one ear missing. It looked out of place amongst all the machinery and tools.

Tammy saw what she was looking at and

gave her a wobbly smile. "It's Cindy's favourite bear. I keep it there to remind me of her. Now," she clapped her hands and shook herself. "You must be thirsty," she said. "All we have is water I'm afraid, but I'll fetch you some." She hurried out of the workshop.

Jade was about to see if she wanted help, but Tim rushed in, panic painted across his pale face. "Girls! Quick!" he said in a frantic, hushed voice. "Someone's coming! Hide, and I'll try to keep them out!" He hurriedly closed the workshop door behind him.

Jade grabbed Pearl and pulled her behind a machine that looked like a cross between a lawnmower and a huge pair of scissors. Coral

crawled under the workbench while Topaz and Opal hid behind one of the other machines.

Jade felt her heart thumping against her ribs.

Pearl put her hand to her ear and shook her head. "I don't hear—"

Jade shushed her, but Pearl was right. No sounds were coming from outside – maybe whoever it was had gone away. She waited a moment longer before exchanging a look with Topaz, who was hiding behind a machine with lots of metal arms.

"I think the coast is clear," whispered Topaz.

Just then, the door opened and Tim looked inside. Jade smiled at him. "Have they gone?" she asked him.

But Tim's expression changed. "I'm sorry," he said, then slammed the workshop door shut with a heavy metallic thud.

"Wait!" cried Jade, her arm outstretched.

But it was too late. The girls heard the sliding of metal on metal as heavy bolts locked the door. They were trapped!

Chapter 4

"No!" yelled Coral. She scrambled out from under the workbench, ran to the door and pounded on it with both her fists.

"Let us out!" cried Topaz. She joined Coral and hammered so hard with her super-strength that her hands dented the thick metal.

Opal stood beside her, banging the door too. "Maybe he's locked us in for safety," she said. But she bit her lip, unsure.

Unfortunately, Jade *was* sure. She had seen the expression on Tim's face, somewhere

between shame and sorrow. He'd locked them in to trap them.

From the other side of the door came the muffled sound of Tim's voice. "I-I-I'm so sorry ..."

"Tim!" his wife cried. "You can't!"

"I have to save Cindy," Tim replied. "I'm going to hand them over to Obsidian!"

Jade shut her eyes and took a deep breath.

"No!" Tammy exclaimed. "I miss Cindy too, but there has to be another way! Come back, Tim!"

Jade heard another door clang and then there was silence. Tim and Tammy must have gone into their house, and if Tammy couldn't change her husband's mind, they were sitting ducks for Obsidian to capture.

Jade clenched her fist angrily. But it wasn't Tammy's fault. It wasn't even Tim's fault. This was Obsidian's fault for making the people so desperate.

In the distance Jade heard howling wolves – Snarl and Menace!

"They sound hungry," said Coral. "Opal, what are they saying?"

Opal's magical power was speaking to animals – she could even understand the dreadful wolves. "Uh-oh," she said, her eyes wide. "They're saying that they've picked up our trail!"

"Come on, girls, we have to get out of here!" exclaimed Topaz. She grabbed the large door handle and pulled it. If anything was going to get the door open, it was her super-strength. The handle buckled and bent. The other girls joined in too. Five pairs of hands all pulled ... until the handle snapped off! The girls fell to the floor in a pile of legs and arms.

Jade had seen the thick bolts as they slid across. She closed her eyes and there it was – the blueprint she needed.

"There's no way to force the door open," she told the others as she stood up. "There are six bolts."

The girls looked up at her from the floor, their faces full of disappointment.

"But that's OK," she said, "because I have a key ..."

Pearl tilted her head to the side. "Huh? How?"

"Or at least, I will do." Jade looked around the room, trying to find the objects she needed. "Can someone hand me those things that look like a pair of tweezers, please?"

"Here!" said Coral, throwing them over.

Jade took apart the engine of the machine she had been hiding behind and found two thin metal strips. She ripped them out before bending them into shape. Then she hunted the shelves for the other parts she needed, before fitting them all together, following the blueprint in her head.

"Fingers crossed," she said, wincing as she looked at her friends.

Eight hands went into the air, fingers crossed.

Jade inserted her makeshift key into the lock. She turned the handle and heard the bent metal moving around in the lock. Then a click, then another click, then the same metallic clunk they'd heard when the door had opened before.

Jade grinned at her friends. "Open sesame ..." She pulled at what was left of the handle and the door opened with ease.

"You're amazing!" said Coral.

"Well done, Jade," said Pearl, jumping up and down. Topaz put a congratulatory hand on her shoulder. Opal gave her a thumbs up, beaming from ear to ear.

The girls hurried out the door, but Jade hesitated for a moment. "Do you think it's bad if I take a few tools?" she asked the others. "I think

we might need them."

"Of course not!" said Topaz. "We can bring them back later."

There was a tool belt on the workbench and Jade wrapped it round her waist. Then she carefully chose some tools and put them in the belt's loops and pockets. She was about to leave when she spotted Cindy's bear on the high shelf. On a whim, she reached up, took it down and tucked it into her belt. She made a silent promise that she would find Cindy and give her the bear.

Jade followed her friends down a small side street, then into a larger road which was lined with rust-covered shops and houses. The wolves howled somewhere behind them – they sounded close.

"I think they've found the workshop," said Opal.

Jade looked around hurriedly. All she could

see on the other side of the road were small, dead-end alleyways. In front of them a bridge crossed a wide, fast-flowing river. The bridge was mechanical, each half lifting up and down to let boats through, but now it was stuck part-way so there was a wide gap in the middle.

Topaz pointed at it. "Think we could make that jump?"

"Easy-peasy," said Jade.

They scrambled up the half-raised bridge. Jade leapt across the gap first, trying not to think about the water below. She landed on the other side, grabbing tightly to the top of the bridge to stop herself slipping down the other side. Her friends followed after

her – Opal almost fell backwards into the water, but Jade caught her arm just in time. Then, one by one, the girls slid down to the bottom of the bridge.

On the opposite side, their faces scrunched

up with fury, appeared Larry and Boil, their
wolves in front of them, straining at their leashes.

Obsidian's henchmen hurried up the sloping
bridge after the girls. Boil puffed as he clambered
up the steep incline. Larry and his wolf jumped

first, Larry's long, lanky legs scissoring over the gap with ease. Boil jumped but fell short. His wolf made it to the other side, leaving Boil dangling from the bridge by the leash. "Laaarry!" he wailed, his legs kicking and thrashing in the air. "Help!"

"I guess Boil just wants to hang around," giggled Pearl. Jade put her hand to her mouth to stifle her laughter.

"You oaf!" Larry cried, huffing and puffing as he slowly pulled Boil up to the top of the bridge.

While the two men were distracted the girls ran, sprinting down several streets until the bridge was out of sight. They stopped by a small stream that fed into the main river, and collapsed into laughter.

"Larry and Boil are no match for us," said Topaz.

"No," said Opal, "but I wouldn't want to come face to teeth with one of those wolves."

Jade was pleased they'd given the men the slip, but they had to get moving.

"How will we find Jasper?" asked Coral, twirling her hair nervously.

"I've been thinking about that," said Topaz, "and I think I've come up with something."

The girls all looked at her expectantly.

"Jasper said he'd been spying on Obsidian and she was close to finding the Treasure, right?" said Topaz. "That means we need to follow the map to the Treasure and we'll be on the same path as Jasper."

"Brilliant!" said Jade. "And once we have Jasper and the gemstone safe, we'll track down the missing children!"

The girls gathered round Jade. As soon as she held the map the stone in her ring started to glow, just the same as Topaz's had done on the Orange Isle. Then a glowing X appeared on the map too – it seemed to be in the tower that stood in the centre of the island. Jade wondered if the tower was the palace – her home when she was a baby. Her stomach did a flip thinking about the family she'd never know. *Were they nice people? Did they love her? Were they kind to the people of the Green Isle?*

"Hang on a second," Opal said, reaching out towards the map. She touched it and the place where she touched enlarged – a wonderful magical feature of the map.

"Look," gasped Jade, pointing at the map, "a tunnel!"

"It looks like there are lots of them," said Pearl.

"I bet those are engineering tunnels," Jade said, thinking like a mechanic. "They're in the places where electricity and steam are needed to power the buildings above."

"So if we find the right tunnel, it'll take us inside the tower," said Topaz.

Jade nodded. They all studied the map.

"Look!" said Jade. She traced a tunnel with her finger. "This is the tunnel we need – and it goes right under where we're standing."

"Perfect!" said Opal. "But how do we get into it?"

The five friends fell silent as they thought about what to do. The only sound was the trickle of water. Because of her phobia, Jade couldn't ignore the noise ... then she saw where it was coming from. In a wall beside the stream was a grate. And the grate led to a ...

"Look, the entrance!" Jade said, pointing it

out to the other girls.

"What are we waiting for?" asked Coral.

Topaz used her super-strength to remove the rusty grate so the girls could step inside. Steep, damp steps led down into a tunnel with a gutter of water that trickled along the bottom.

It's not too much water, Jade thought. *I can handle it.*

After all, this tunnel led to the tower. There they might find Jasper, the gemstone and the children. The island would be safe in no time!

Chapter 5

It took a few moments for Jade's eyes to adjust to the darkness of the tunnel. Grates in the ceiling let in bars of sunlight. The tunnel was big, high enough to stand in, and wide enough so that Jade could stretch out both arms and not touch the sides. Clean, too – made of polished steel. The girls walked carefully through the shallow trickle of water that flowed along the floor, trying to make as little noise as possible.

Before they had gone far, the tunnel forked into two. Opal looked at the map and pointed

them down the left tunnel. But then she stopped the group with one raised hand. "Wait ... did you hear that?" she asked.

"Hear what?" Jade asked. The only thing she heard was their splashing footsteps and the pulsing of her heart in her ears.

"I didn't hear anything," said Pearl.

"Me neither," said Coral.

"Must be an animal," said Topaz, "if only Opal can hear it."

"I'll be right back," Opal said, and she scurried down the right-hand tunnel. But the other girls weren't going to let Opal go off on her own, and they followed her.

"Someone's crying for help," Opal told them, as they made their way further into the darkness.

Eventually, the tunnel opened up into a gigantic, circular room, the top of which was too high to see clearly. Cogs, wheels, pipes and rods

criss-crossed above their heads, and a massive vat – the size of a house – loomed in the centre of the room. Jade realised what they were looking at. The vat must be filled with water, which the furnace beneath it heated to create steam. *It must power the entire island!* she thought. But the furnace was covered in dusty cobwebs and obviously hadn't been lit for a long time.

"Where are you?" Opal called out.

This time Jade heard it too – a tiny, sad barking sound. She looked up and saw a little fox cub standing on a platform high above them. Jade

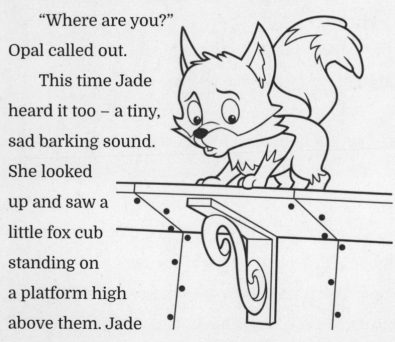

thought he looked worried; he paced nervously back and forth and his eyes were opened very wide.

"Are you OK?" Opal asked him.

The fox barked in reply.

"He says he's stuck," Opal told the girls.

"He's so cute!" said Coral.

"Come on then," said Opal, opening her arms out wide.

"Jump," said Pearl, jumping up and down to demonstrate. "We'll catch you."

But the fox cub backed away from the edge. It seemed he didn't like the sound of jumping.

"How are we going to get him down?" Coral wondered.

Jade stepped forward. "Opal, please tell the cub that I'm the princess of this island – Princess Jade." She did her best to sound regal. Pearl giggled beside her. "And as a magical princess, there's no way I'd ever let anything happen to him." Jade opened her arms and positioned herself directly below the platform's edge.

Opal repeated what Jade had said and the fox cub stepped forward. He hesitated one last time before leaping into the air. Jade caught him easily. He licked her hands and face happily.

"Got you!" she said, giving the little creature a hug before placing him on the floor. "But I'm afraid we can't take you out of these tunnels – we have a wicked witch to battle. Do you feel like an adventure?"

Opal used her power to ask the cub Jade's question and he barked back confidently. "He says bring it on!" she translated. The five friends laughed happily and turned back into the tunnel they had come from, accompanied by their new animal friend.

"Funny how he could be scared of jumping

down," said Topaz, "but not scared of tackling a horrible witch."

The others giggled but Jade totally understood. *Give me a cutlass and a fight with Obsidian over a pool of water any day,* she thought to herself.

Suddenly, there was a terrifying booming sound. It came from the heating room. The girls all whirled around to face it, and Jade's heart thundered as a massive ball of flame rushed up the tunnel towards them.

"Fireball!" shouted Topaz. "Everyone down!"

But as Jade, Topaz, Pearl, Opal and even the fox cub dropped to their fronts and flattened themselves against the wet floor, Coral stood and turned towards the fire.

"Oh no," said Coral, wagging her finger as if talking to a naughty toddler and not a ball of flames. "No way!" She held out her hands and even from her place on the floor, Jade could feel the icy blast. The fireball disappeared in an instant!

"Quick thinking, Coral!" Jade said, jumping up and giving her a hug.

Coral curtsied in response. "What's the point in controlling the elements if you can't put out a few flames once in a while?" she said with a grin.

"That furnace looked like it hadn't been used in years," said Jade. "I wonder why it just started up again?"

"I'll give you one guess," said Topaz frowning furiously.

"Obsidian!" chorused the other four.

"She must know where we are," said Opal gritting her teeth. The fox cub shuddered.

"Obsidian is playing dirty!" said Jade, angrily. "But she can't stop us."

Jade led the girls onward, following the

map, but when the tunnel rounded a corner she stopped in dismay: the tunnel grew bigger, but the bottom half of it sloped down into a deep pool of dark water. Above the water the tunnel was blocked by a solid-looking metal grate.

"Let me try," said Topaz, wading out into the chest-deep water. She yanked and pushed at the grate, but even with her super-strength, she couldn't shift it. Topaz took a deep breath and disappeared under the water. She emerged, spluttering, a few seconds later. "There's a gap underneath the grate," she said. "It's narrow, but I think we can swim through it."

Jade swallowed hard. The only way through was by fully submerging herself in the water. While the others wasted no time splashing in, Jade started to tremble.

"What about the fox cub?" she asked.

"We could pass him through the grate," said

Coral. "Come on, Jade."

But Jade felt faint. She doubled over to stop her head from spinning.

"What's the matter?" asked Pearl.

Jade looked up to see the worried faces of her friends. Could she tell them? She wasn't even sure they'd want to be her friend any more. "You're going to think I'm so silly," she said.

"Try us," said Topaz.

Jade burst into tears. "I'm scared of water! Terrified! Even this little pool of water! I just can't do it."

She watched as her four friends' mouths fell open.

"It's true," she said. "I should just go back to Breakwater Hall. I'm the worst princess pirate ever."

The others exchanged glances with each other, and then rushed forward so fast Jade

thought they'd knock her over. But instead they wrapped her into the biggest, warmest hug she'd ever received.

"Why didn't you say?" asked Topaz.

"It's perfectly natural to be scared of water!" added Opal.

"This explains a lot," said Pearl. "Like why you didn't sign up to any swimming races on sports day."

"And how you turn that pretty shade of green when anyone mentions sailing," Coral added.

Topaz shook her head in disbelief. "So you've been sailing the high seas in Lemuria, and sailing on Lapis Lake at school, and all the time you were scared?"

Jade nodded. "Do you still want me to be in your crew?" she asked nervously, looking at the ground in front of her boots.

"Are you kidding?!" answered Topaz. "You're

now officially the bravest person I know!"

Jade gave a wobbly smile. She was so lucky to have friends who would always stick by her.

"I'm glad you told us," said Opal, her hand still on Jade's shoulder.

"Do you feel better now?" asked Pearl.

Jade nodded. She felt as if someone had taken a heavy bag off her back.

"Don't you worry," Topaz said. "Together we'll help you. We'll swim under the grate and get it open from the other side."

"Yes," said Pearl. "Then I'll come back for you and the fox cub. I'll give you both a piggyback so you hardly touch the water."

"Are you sure?" said Jade, amazed that her friends would go to all this trouble to help her deal with her fear.

"Of course!" smiled Coral.

"All friends on deck, remember," said Topaz.

"Here, take the map," said Opal, passing it to Jade. "And him too," she added, picking up the fox cub and placing him on Jade's shoulder. The cub's soft tail and snuffly breathing felt so comforting. Jade watched as her friends dived under the water, Pearl's legs shimmering as they turned into her tail. She was the first to emerge at the other side of the locked gate, followed soon after by the others. They made it look easy, but just watching them had Jade's stomach in knots.

"Everyone OK?" she asked.

Pearl gave a thumbs up. "And this grate should be easy to open," she said. "Just a couple of bolts."

"Bit rusty though," frowned Opal.

Topaz treaded water, reached up to the bolts, and pushed them across with ease. She held the grate open as Pearl swam back for Jade and the cub. Jade wrapped her arms around Pearl's

shoulders and her legs around her waist, and Pearl – true to her word – made sure that Jade stayed dry above the water. As Pearl reached shallow water her tail became legs, and she bent forward to let Jade step off on to dry ground again. The cub gave a happy yip as it bounded down from Jade's shoulder.

"Thanks so much, girls," Jade said to them. Apart from her, they were all dripping wet. "I'd hug you but ... you're soaking!"

The others laughed.

"Not far to go now," Jade said. From the look of the map, they just had to climb some stairs and then they'd reach the inside of the tower. Jade set off at a jog, the others following close behind.

But before they reached the stairs they found themselves in a room with two doors leading in different directions. Jade tried to examine the map to work out which one to choose. But it was

too dark to see. Jade could only just make out the silhouettes of her friends.

"Where now, Jade?" asked Topaz. "Left or right?"

But all Jade could see was the glowing X on the map. "I can't quite ..."

"Hey," said Pearl, "there's a switch here. Let me try ..."

But Jade's genius power told her it was no light switch.

"Pearl! No!" she shouted. But it was too late. With a whoosh and a clunk a portcullis slammed down across the middle of the room.

Jade had fallen backwards on one side of the portcullis, and she found to her horror that her four friends and the little fox cub were all on the other side. She was trapped ... or they were!

Pearl tried to flip the switch back, but nothing happened. "What have I done?" cried Pearl. "I'm

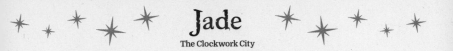

so sorry!"

"You were just trying to help," Coral told her.

Opal put her arms through the bars and held Jade's hands. "We'll get you out of there," she said.

Topaz tried everything she could to lift the portcullis ... but it wouldn't budge.

"Argggh!" yelled Topaz in frustration. "What do we do now?"

Jade took a deep breath and told herself to be brave. She looked at the map again and, now that her eyes had adjusted, she could just see that the door on the other side of the portcullis led to the glowing X. "Take the map," she said, thrusting it through the bars. "You should go on without me."

"We should stay together," said Coral, her voice quavering in the gloom.

"The most important thing is finding the Treasure," Jade said, sounding more confident

than she felt. "I'll head through this door and see where it leads. You four take the other door."

"Only if you're sure," said Topaz.

"Certain," Jade said with a nod. "Meet back at Nestor."

Jade squeezed her friends' hands through the bars and said goodbye. She had felt alone for most of her life, but as she watched her friends run out of the door, shouting their promises to find her again, she'd never felt more lonely.

Chapter 6

J ade took a deep breath.

I can do this.

She pushed the door open to find a light-filled spiral staircase. With her genius power, Jade could see these stairs should work like an escalator, only they were covered in the same rust that smothered the whole island. The stairs were steep and soon Jade's legs ached as she took step after step. *If only the mechanism that powered these stairs was working now!* she thought.

Occasionally Jade reached a landing and a locked door. *What lay behind these doors?* she wondered. This was her family home, the home that Jade was born in and lived in as a baby. Jade pressed higher and higher – she had to get to the top of the tower to see if there was any sign of the Treasure, the children, or Jasper. As she stopped to catch her breath she thought she heard a faint whirring noise coming from somewhere above.

At the next landing Jade reached, the door was unlocked and ajar. Jade stepped inside cautiously. The room was circular, like the dorm she shared with the girls at Breakwater Hall. A beautiful stained-glass window took up most of one wall, and a mechanical baby's crib stood in front of it. The crib rocked jerkily back-and-forth – that's what the whirring noise was! Above the crib was a mobile with boats, ships, fish and an octopus. Jade wondered if this had been her crib and whether she'd stared up at that mobile when she was a tiny baby.

Opposite the crib, three shelves were built cleverly into the circular wall. Each shelf was crammed with toys: teddy bears, miniature tool kits, a set of train tracks. Jade approached them with a smile on her face. *If this was my room then these would have been the perfect toys for me.* She knew she should be moving on, but told herself she needed to get her breath back for a minute.

In the centre of the middle shelf was a beautiful box with a silver clasp on the front. Jade touched it and saw her ring glow green for an instant. *It must have been mine!* she thought. Jade realised with surprise that this was the only metallic thing she'd seen that didn't have any rust on it. The box had to be protected in some way.

She unlocked the clasp of the box and the lid flipped open. Inside a little scene was set: a man and a woman, both with jet-black hair made of string and green eyes made of tiny gemstones, and both wearing crowns. They each held the hand of a little girl, also with black hair and green eyes. *I've never seen anything so beautiful,* Jade thought.

Jade carefully picked up the box and found a tiny handle at the back. It was a music box! As soon as she cranked it the people in the scene started to move. They walked along, their legs striding so realistically that if Jade blurred her eyes she could have been watching a film of real people. Behind them, tiny lights made it look like they were walking through real streets. The queen pointed at things while the king waved at people that weren't there. Then both figures bent down and kissed the little girl.

All of this scene unfolded to music, and Jade noticed she was humming along. It was a lullaby, both sad and happy at the same time.  Of course! It was the same tune she always hummed when she was nervous. If she hadn't been sure of it before, she was certain now. *This had once been her room. This was how she'd known this tune all her life.*

As soon as the music finished and the three figures had gone back to their original positions, there was a *clunk-click* noise, and a little drawer flew open, making Jade jump and cry out in surprise.

Inside the drawer was a folded piece of paper. Jade held her breath. She'd been there when Topaz had read a note from her parents – could this be something similar? Jade picked up the paper and took a deep breath, preparing herself. She unfolded the paper, and there, in beautiful green handwriting, was a letter.

Dearest Jade,

Knowing we'll never see you again is the worst thing we've ever had to face. Knowing you'll one day read this, alive and well and hopefully happy, is the only thing that makes parting from you possible.

It is your duty, as princess of this wonderful island, to save the people and stop Obsidian forever. You will have to be brave, but we know you have it in you. Even as a tiny baby, you were always so strong.

But saving the people is not your only task in life. You must be happy, you must laugh and have fun, and above all, you must make a new family – wherever you find yourself. Because family is the most important thing in the world.

All our love,
Mum and Dad

Jade paused and wiped the tears from her eyes. Reading this letter from her parents was hard, but it also made her smile, because instantly she thought of her friends: Topaz, Opal,

Coral and Pearl. They were her family now. Her island was broken but Jade knew better than anyone that anything could be fixed with the right tools and a bit of hard work. Well, she and her princess friends were the tools for the job and they weren't going to stop until they'd defeated Obsidian once and for all.

***

Jade stood tall. Thinking of the others made her remember her mission. She wiped the last tear from her cheek, pocketed the music box carefully in her tool belt, and cast one last glance at the place where she was born before running up the remaining stairs. Her legs didn't hurt any more, knowing her parents loved her filled her with strength and energy. Knowing that she had a new family made her stronger than iron.

At last Jade reached the top of the stairs and entered a huge room. The walls were stainless

steel, and two silver thrones sat at the far end.

"The throne room!" she gasped.

A beautiful mechanical clock in a tall metal case stood in the corner. But it was covered in rust and had clearly stopped years ago. The walls were covered in etchings and glinted green with tiny jade stones that were set into the design. There were four windows looking out – north, south, east and west – and in front of each window was a telescope.

Perfect! thought Jade. *From here I'll be able to see the whole island!* She raced over to the nearest telescope and put her eye to the lens. But all she saw were brown smudges – it was rusted inside!

"Argh!" she yelled in frustration.

But Jade knew she mustn't give up. Maybe one of the other telescopes was working ...

A muffled noise stopped her in her tracks.

"Hello?" she said nervously.

The muffled noise sounded again, this time slightly louder.

It sounded like it was coming from the balcony. Jade took down a silver sword that was hanging from the wall and followed the noise cautiously. It could be a trap set by Obsidian. She pushed the glass and metal doors open and what she saw made her gasp.

"Jasper!" she shouted.

Jasper was in a cage, his mouth covered in a gag, his hands tied behind his back. The cage was made of thick metal bars, locked shut with a heavy padlock. Jasper's parrot, Pegleg, was gagged too, with his wings tied tightly to his sides. All Jade could hear were muffled sounds, but from Jasper's smiling eyes and the way Pegleg hopped around, Jade could tell they were happy to see her.

"I'm so glad I've found you!" she said. "We got your note and …"

But she trailed off when she saw that the cage wasn't their biggest problem. It was dangling off the edge of the balcony, suspended in mid-air by a mechanical arm.

"We'd better get you out of there," said Jade. Jasper nodded frantically.

Jade peered over the edge of the balcony to see what lay below. It wasn't the height so much that scared her – it was the watery moat Jasper would fall into if the cage were to drop. Jade swallowed down a massive lump of fear.

"Don't worry," she said. "I'll find something to pick the lock." She'd picked a lock earlier when they'd been trapped in the workshop. This padlock should be easy to open too … she hoped. Jade closed her eyes and saw the blueprint of a key – the exact shape she'd need to open the

lock. She just needed to find something to make it out of. There was one thing she could use ... but Jade hoped she'd be able to find something else instead.

The sound of footsteps made Jade spin on her heel.

Looking back into the room, Jade saw Obsidian enter, swishing her cloak. Lightning crackled from the black stone in her staff. Behind her appeared Larry and Boil – Boil red-faced and puffing from climbing the steps.

Jade raised the sword in her hand. "Go away, Obsidian," she shouted. "Leave me and my island alone."

"Not a chance," Obsidian sneered. "Hand over the Treasure and map, or your little friend will die. And so will that mangy parrot!"

Chapter 7

Jade narrowed her eyes and glared at Obsidian.

"I haven't got the map," Jade told her. "It's safely with my friends. And hopefully the Treasure is now, too. But even if I did have them, I wouldn't give them to you."

Obsidian threw back her head and cackled. "Your friends," she sneered, "have deserted you. I saw them jump back on to that stupid ship of yours and sail off towards the horizon. They've abandoned you."

Jade's heart glowed like her ring. "Now I

know you're lying," she told Obsidian, a smile on her face. "My friends would never abandon me. You're lying because you're scared we're going to beat you ... which we will."

Obsidian gritted her teeth. "Scared?! I'll show you!" She lunged forward and shot a blast of lightning at the chain that Jasper and Pegleg's cage swung from. The chain exploded into pieces and Jasper let out a muffled yell as the cage dropped out of sight. Jade's stomach dropped with it. She rushed to the edge of the balcony and got there in time to see the splash so far below that she barely heard the sound it made.

"No!" Jade cried, her eyes filling with tears. Jasper and Pegleg would drown!

Obsidian cackled cruelly. Larry and Boil laughed too and even their wolves howled in approval. "You speak of friends. Well, without this ..." she pulled out a gold key and waved it in the air, "your little friend will be dead within a minute. Tell me where to find the Treasure and ..."

But Jade wasn't listening. She closed her eyes and focused on the blueprint in her mind. The pieces she needed to make a key were right in her pocket, and now she had no choice but to use them. She put the cutlass in her belt and pulled out the music box. She took a deep breath, knowing Jasper and Pegleg were more important even than this precious gift from her parents, and snapped the music box in half. Then she turned to the balcony's edge once more. She thought of the letter, how her mum and dad had told her to be brave, and summoned all her courage.

"Where do you think you're going?" Obsidian cried out. "Release the wolves!"

Larry and Boil let Snarl and Menace loose. That was all the incentive Jade needed. She threw herself head first over the edge of the balcony.

The fall seemed to take hours, when really it must have been seconds. Hitting the water felt like hitting a brick wall and knocked the breath right out of her. But as soon as she could, Jade started kicking for the surface. Already her hands were at work.

Jasper's cage was next to her, his eyes and messy brown hair just visible above the surface. Pegleg was on Jasper's shoulder, his beak held up so he could breathe. Thankfully, the cage hadn't sunk immediately, which gave Jade a little time. She trod water as best she could, thankful that she was in a calm moat instead of the open ocean. But that didn't stop the fear that was

threatening to overwhelm her.

Looking at the two halves of her music box, Jade pulled out the parts she needed – a long wire, a cog and a hook – and used the tools from her belt to fashion a key, following the blueprint in her mind. But making the key was the easy part. She was already dreading what she'd have to do next: dive down into the water again.

Come on, Jade, she told herself. *You've got to do this. You're the only one who can save Jasper and Pegleg.*

Jade took a deep breath, her legs already burning from treading water, and dived beneath the surface.

Below the water, her heartbeat was so loud she could hear it in her ears. The cage was slowly sinking deeper and deeper. Jasper was completely underwater now, his face turning red from holding his breath, frantically trying to work

himself out of his bound hands. He hadn't given up, and Jade wasn't about to either.

As Jasper saw Jade his eyes opened wide in delight. He had managed to free his hands and now undid the rope that tied Pegleg's wings. Jade pulled herself down to the padlock on the door. Her legs kept floating upwards so she wrapped them tightly around the bars of the cage.

She pushed in her makeshift key. It didn't like the resistance against the water, but with a strong push, the key turned and opened the padlock. Jade let the padlock fall to the bottom of the moat and pulled open the door.

Bubbles escaped out of Jasper's mouth and Jade could tell that he couldn't hold his breath much longer. She grabbed Jasper by the hand and he held on to Pegleg with his other hand. They both kicked for the surface, Jasper's face turning blue as he ran out of oxygen. Jade was

running out of air too, but finally they broke through the surface. Jade gasped, gulping down a lungful of air. Jasper opened his mouth wide, the rasping noise he made letting Jade know he'd been seconds away from passing out. Pegleg looked weakest of all. Jade took him from Jasper and trod water as she rubbed the feathers on poor Pegleg's little chest.

"Come on, Pegleg!" she shouted desperately. "Wake up!"

Eventually Pegleg opened his eyes and gave out a pathetic chirp.

"Pegleg!" Jade cried, and for a moment her fear of the water was gone and all she felt was relief. She'd saved them both!

"Jade jump, Jade jump," Pegleg wheezed, as he nuzzled his beak into her chin.

"Anything for you, little guy," she said.

The friends swam to the side of the moat.

Jade used the last of her strength to
pull Jasper out after
her. He lay on his
back panting. "Dry
land," spluttered Jade,
"I could kiss it!"

Jasper gave a last cough and
turned to face Jade. "Landlubber," he grinned.

Jade laughed. "You've got me."

Jasper's smile dropped and he looked Jade
in the eye. "Then that makes what you just did
the bravest thing I've ever seen anyone do. Thank
you so much, Jade."

Jade felt herself blush with pride. She took
out the broken music box that she'd stuffed in
her tool belt. She hoped her parents wouldn't
mind that she destroyed it to save her friend. She
hoped they'd be proud of her too.

"Quick question," Jasper said, as Jade put

the music box back in her belt. "What's with the bear?" He pointed to the teddy tucked into Jade's belt.

"Long story," Jade told him sadly. "But I have to return it to a little girl."

She'd saved Jasper but now they needed to find the Treasure and the children. The palace walls rose high around them but Jade spotted the entrance to a little tunnel in the wall not far from where they were sitting.

"The others have the map," she told Jasper. "They're looking for the gemstone. Do you know where it is?"

"Find the gemstone," squawked Pegleg, his voice a little weaker than usual.

Jasper sighed heavily, still not quite recovered from his ordeal. "All I know is the Treasure's very close," he said, staggering to his feet. "Well, what are we waiting for?" He stumbled forward and Jade jumped up to catch him. Together, they reached the entrance to the tunnel, before pulling back the broken grate and hurrying inside.

And as the grate clanked shut behind them, Jade thought she heard a frustrated scream from Obsidian high above them. It sounded like, "I'll get you, princesses!"

But Jade didn't care. She'd like to see her try.

Chapter 8

Jade and Jasper hurried down the tunnel that led from the moat, with Pegleg flying after them. The friends came to a stop when the tunnel split into two. Jade looked both ways. "I have no idea where we're going," she admitted. "Without the map, we could be lost down here for hours!"

Jasper pulled a gold coin out of one of his soaked trouser pockets. "Heads for left, tails for right," he said with a grin.

Jade grinned back. It was as good a way as any. "Tails!" she said.

Jasper tossed the coin into the air. As she watched it spin, Jade heard a tapping noise, like someone drumming their fingers on metal. Jasper heard it too and he turned in the direction the noise was coming from. The coin clattered to the floor.

The tapping noise grew louder. Then from behind a tangle of pipes, they saw a little black nose, followed by a red furry body, and a bushy tail. Pegleg squawked in alarm.

"Speaking of tails!" said Jade, beaming. "Don't worry, Pegleg, this fox cub is our friend."

The cub ran straight over to them and rubbed against Jade's legs to greet her. "I'm pleased to see you too," she smiled down at him. "Do you know where the others are? I wish I could understand you like Opal can."

The cub ran behind Jade and nudged her in the direction he'd appeared from. Then he grabbed hold of Jasper's trouser leg and pulled Jasper the same way. Jade and Jasper laughed.

"I think that's pretty clear!" Jade said.

They followed the cub through the maze of tunnels that snaked under the city. Jade hoped he was leading them to her friends. Then, from around a corner, they heard familiar voices.

"We need Jade," Topaz was saying.

"So we're stuck until we find her," replied Pearl, sounding hopeless, "or until she finds us."

Jade jumped around the corner. "Did someone call for the princess of the Green Isle?" she shouted with a grin.

"Jade!" the girls cried together. "Jasper!"

"You're here!" Pearl said, jumping up and down.

Pegleg squawked happily.

"And hello to you too, Pegleg," said Opal.

"Good to see you," added Topaz.

Jade gave Opal a hug. "Thanks for sending this little guy to find us," she said, gesturing at the fox cub.

Opal pushed Jade away from her with a grimace. "Ew ... how come you're all wet?" she asked.

"Oh, sorry!" Jade laughed.

"Jade was amazing!" Jasper said, before telling them all how Jade had confronted Obsidian and then jumped from the top of the tower to save him and Pegleg. "Then she somehow made a key ... while she was underwater!"

Her friends' mouths fell open.

"That's unbelievable," said Topaz. "Especially since you're so scared of water. Well done!"

"I'm so sorry we weren't there to help you," said Opal, putting her hand on Jade's shoulder.

"That's OK," said Jade. "Obsidian tried to convince me you'd gone. But I knew you'd never leave me alone. *All friends on deck,* right?"

Her friends smiled at her. "I don't care how wet you are," said Coral, squeezing her tight. "I'm giving you a hug!"

"Now what's the problem?" asked Jade, once Coral had let go of her.

"We followed the map," explained Topaz, "but we're at a dead end." She pointed to a closed door in front of them. "The Treasure should be just behind here ... but it looks like only your ring can unlock the door."

Jade saw the small hole next to the door that Topaz was talking about. It was an oval shape – the exact shape of the stone in her ring. Jade put her hand forward, pushed her ring into the hole,

and with a clunk and a whirr, the door slid open.

"Woohoo!" whooped Coral.

They all rushed through the door.

It was a room about the size of a classroom, but every wall was covered with switches and buttons, joysticks and levers.

"Where's the gemstone?" Topaz wondered aloud.

There were ten dust-covered TV screens on one of the walls and a chair in front of them. Jade wiped the dust off one of the screens. The image was of the furnace that had shot the fireball at them earlier. Another screen showed the greenhouses full of wilted plants. A third showed Nestor sitting in the harbour.

"Hi, Nestor!" Pearl said, waving.

Nestor seemed to be dozing, his eyes closed, deep in slumber.

"I think this is the control room for all the

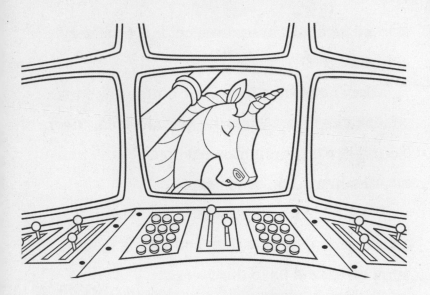

machinery on the island," said Jade, impressed by all of the inventions and machinery she could see on the screens.

Pearl and Coral were messing around with the controls. "Let's see if we can wake Nestor," Pearl said, pressing a button. The button made a beeping noise.

Coral giggled and pressed another button. It made another beep, this one high-pitched. "One of these has to work the docking system." Pulling a lever made yet another beep, this time very deep.

Jade pressed a few of the buttons and then she had an idea. "Those beeps," she said, "they sound like different musical notes."

"I suppose so," said Jasper.

"I think it's a code," said Jade. "I bet if we played the right tune then something would happen to lead us to the Treasure."

"But what's the tune?" Topaz asked.

Pegleg squawked a sea shanty.

"I don't think that's it, Pegleg," laughed Opal, stroking the parrot on the head.

Jade knew exactly what the tune would be. She went over to the main control panel and pressed buttons and pulled levers until she heard every note she needed. Then she began to play the tune: the tune that had been stuck in her head for as long as she could remember.

"Is that the song you were singing at sports day?" asked Opal.

Jade nodded. "It's the song my parents used to sing to me," she told them. "They left me a music box." She pulled out the broken pieces of the music box from her tool belt. Topaz took them and examined the fragments. "I had to break it to make ..." Jade looked at Jasper, she didn't want to make him feel bad by telling him she'd broken it for him. Instead she continued, "I broke it to

make something. But it doesn't matter. I'll never forget the tune."

She played it on the buttons and levers perfectly. A lullaby, both sad and happy at the same time. Then, when the tune finished, they waited. All of them held their breath. Even the fox cub was silent.

A tiny whirring noise broke the silence. Jade turned and noticed a small hatch, no larger than a book, at the base of the wall. It was opening! Jade saw a flash of green and leapt towards it. Jasper and the other girls crowded around her.

"The gemstone!" whispered Topaz.

Jade bent down to pick it up. The stone fitted snugly into her hands. A beautiful green gemstone in an oval shape, made out of jade. Her ring glinted as if talking to it.

"You did it, Jade!" said Pearl.

"You've saved the island!" Jasper cheered,

patting her on the back.

"*We* did it," said Jade, grinning so much that her mouth hurt. "But we haven't saved the island quite yet. We need to take the Treasure up to the throne room to make the magic work."

"Come on, then," said Opal, giving the map a quick glance, "what are we waiting for?"

The friends raced out of the door, Pegleg squawking, "Save the Green Isle, save the Green Isle," as they went.

Chapter 9

J ade was following the others up the steps that led to the throne room when a thought suddenly hit her.

"Stop!" she called out.

Her friends stopped and turned to her, puzzled frowns on their faces.

"We have to save the children first," explained Jade. "The poor things have been separated from their parents for too long already."

"But we don't know where they are," said Jasper. "I've been here all week and I have no idea."

Opal spoke to the fox cub. "You've been in and out of this palace," she said to him. "Do you know where the children are?"

The little fox cub shook his head sadly.

But looking at the cub had given Jade an idea. "Hey!" she said, pulling the teddy bear out of her belt. "Will you ask the fox to smell this please, Opal?" The bear was wet, but Jade hoped there was still some of Cindy's scent on it. "Perhaps he can lead us to Cindy and the other children."

The fox cub came closer and sniffed the bear all over. He gave a little squeak, then turned and put his nose to the floor.

"He said he's still young," said Opal, "and not the best at picking up scents, but he'll give it a try."

"That's all we ask," said Topaz.

They followed the fox back into the tunnels.

He starting moving faster, his nose never far from the ground, his bushy tail waving behind him.

"Has he found something?" asked Jade, realising that she'd been clenching her fists.

Opal translated the fox's excited yips. "Yes! Down these stairs!"

The friends raced down a narrow stairway, trying to keep up with the fox cub. The stairs were only lit by little flickering lights low down in the walls. When they got to the bottom Jade saw that they'd arrived in a massive room, twice the size of the school hall. Everywhere she looked the walls were lined with bars. Jade saw movement in the dim light behind the bars.

"Is that ...?" she wondered.

Little children were standing up in the cells, their hands reaching through the bars.

"Help!" one child cried out. "Can you help us? Please!"

The noise alerted all the other children, and soon the room was filled with shouting, clapping and cheers.

They'd done it! They'd found the children! Jasper and the girls grinned at each other in delight.

Jade jumped on to an empty crate. "I'm Jade, and these are my friends!" she called out. "We're here to rescue you!"

A gasp came from the cells. "Are you Princess Jade?" asked an older girl. "The ruler of the Green Isle?"

"Are you all princesses?" another girl asked.

"Yup," Coral replied.

"At your service," Pearl added.

The children began to cheer again.

"The saviours of Lemuria!"

"They're here!"

Topaz walked over to a big lever on the wall and pulled it down. Instantly the doors to the cells flung open and the hundreds of children trapped inside came rushing out. The older ones carried the younger ones, and they wasted no time in surrounding the princesses and hugging them. Some curtsied or bowed too.

"Cindy!" Jade shouted. "Is there a Cindy here?"

The crowds parted and a little girl stepped forward nervously. "I'm Cindy," she said, shyly. Her round face was dirty, and Jade noticed tracks on her cheeks from where she'd been crying.

Jade winked at her. "Then this is yours," she

said. "Your mum asked me to give him back to you."

The little girl raced forward, took the bear from Jade and squeezed it tight. "Thank you! Thank you so—"

"Stop right there!"

Jade would know that voice anywhere. She turned to see Obsidian, followed by Larry, Boil and their two drooling wolves. The children screamed as lightning crackled from Obsidian's staff.

"Well, isn't this a cosy scene," said Obsidian, her eyes narrowing. "Princess Jade, I hoped I'd seen the last of you."

Jade shook her head. "Sorry to disappoint, Obsidian. But my friends and I have saved Jasper, found the gemstone, rescued the children, and we're just on our way to save the island too. So if you and your henchmen wouldn't mind getting out of our way—"

Obsidian shot a blast of lightning at the ground where Jade was standing and she had to jump to avoid being hit. She held on tight to the gemstone, already thinking of a plan.

"Coral," she whispered, raising her eyebrows to give her friend a signal. Coral winked and Jade knew she had understood her.

"No one treats my friend like that!" said Coral, taking two steps forward into the room. "Kids," she gestured to the crowd of children behind her, "stand back."

The children gathered in a huddle at the back of the room as Coral stretched out her arms and closed her eyes. A light wind began to blow through the room.

"Your pathetic wind doesn't frighten me!" laughed Obsidian, glaring at her.

"Oh yeah?" answered Coral, her hands still

outstretched. "Then what about a tornado?"

The wind grew stronger and stronger until Jade had to grab on to a pipe at the side of the room to stop herself from falling over. But Obsidian wasn't so quick. The wind caught her billowing cape and blew her backwards. She tried to blast lightning from her staff, but the wind blew it back towards her. The wolves, Larry, and even hefty Boil were powerless against the tornado. The wind pushed them back, back, back, into the cells behind them.

Once Obsidian and her horrible gang were all inside a cell, Topaz lifted the big lever and the bars swung shut, locking them away.

"That should shut you up," said Topaz.

Coral let her arms fall to her sides and the wind stopped at once.

Obsidian hauled herself up and clutched on to the bars. "Let me out!"

Little Cindy stepped up to Obsidian, looked her in the eye, then blew a raspberry.

Jade laughed. "I couldn't have said it better myself."

"Come on, kids," Pearl said to the children. "We have one more thing to do before we take you home."

"What?" asked a little boy, frowning nervously.

"You'll see," said Opal, putting a hand on his shoulder. "And I promise you're going to like it."

The friends ran to the staircase, followed by the children.

"Where do you think you're going?" Obsidian screamed after them.

Jade didn't stop as she answered. "You'll soon find out!"

"So long!" said Pearl with a wave.

Five princess pirates, Jasper, Pegleg, the fox

cub and all of the children of the Green Isle ran up the stairs as fast as they could. There was no rush now, Jade knew that, but she couldn't wait to see the magic happen.

They reached the throne room at the top of the stairs. The others looked around in amazement. But Jade and Jasper had seen the room already and ran straight for the thrones.

"Do you think it'll work like last time?" Jasper asked her.

"Only one way to find out," said Jade.

She stood in front of the thrones, took a deep breath, and held the gemstone out in front of her. She turned and sat on one of the thrones, closing her eyes as she did so. Instantly, the gemstone was gone from her hands and Jade felt a weight on her head – the crown! She smiled. It had worked.

She opened her eyes to see everyone in the

room looking at her.

"It's true," said Cindy. "You *are* the princess!"

Jade nodded. She took the crown off her head and examined it. It was polished silver with five fine points and the bright green gemstone on the front. How beautiful.

The gemstone gave off another green glow and suddenly the air was filled with clicking noises, like someone had let in a thousand crickets. The children all looked around,

confused. The gadgets in the room were clicking back into place, fixing themselves. The mechanical clock started ticking straight away. The rust that covered almost everything simply disappeared. But most amazingly, the roof above them opened up into six different sections like the petals on a flower. They could see the whole island below, and the whole island could see them.

There was a moment's stillness in the city streets as the people – so far below they looked like ants – stopped in shock. Then everything started to move. The train began to puff out steam and run along the tracks. The great fans in the greenhouses began to spin. Bells rang out in the main square. The brown rust disappeared like smoke and the clockwork city was silver and green once more!

A cheer rose from the people below. A cheer

that turned to wails of delight as the children ran to the balcony and waved at their parents below.

"Long live Princess Jade!" the children shouted out.

"Long live Princess Jade!" the grown-ups below shouted back.

Jade blushed. "Aw, come on," she said. "It was nothing."

Her friends gathered round her and gave her a hug. Jade might not have her parents any more, but she had found a family at last.

Chapter 10

"Nestor!" the girls called out.

The bustling dock looked completely different to how it did when they arrived. People were returning to work, releasing their boats from the mechanical docking arms with a touch of a button. All around were happy children hugging their relieved parents.

"Wakey-wakey, Nestor," giggled Pearl.

Nestor shook his mane and gave an indignant cough. "I wasn't sleeping," he said. "Just resting my eyes."

"We believe you," said Opal.

"I won't mention the seagull poop on his head then," Coral whispered.

Nestor lowered the gangplank and they climbed aboard.

"So," came a small voice from the dock, "I'll see you later then."

Jade turned to see that Jasper wasn't following them. He waved sadly from the bottom of the gangplank. Pegleg sat on Jasper's shoulder, waving a wing. Jade ran back down.

"We'll be back," she told him. "We just have to hide this gemstone where Obsidian will never find it." The girls had the perfect hiding place: Breakwater Hall. Obsidian couldn't travel to their world.

"We still have three other islands to rescue," added Topaz. "We'll come back as soon as we can."

"And when we do," said Jade, putting a hand on Jasper's shoulder, "we'll look for your parents." Jasper gave a weak smile and Jade saw tears in his eyes. Obsidian had trapped Jasper's parents somewhere, and seeing all the children reunited with their mums and dads must have made him sad as well as happy.

"Thanks," Jasper said with a sniff. "And thanks for, you know, saving my life and everything. That was really brave."

"All in a day's work for a princess pirate," said Jade, giving a curtsey, salute and then a hug!

The other girls rushed to hug Jasper and Pegleg goodbye too. Then they raced back aboard Nestor and took their positions: Topaz at the helm, Jade at the telescope, the other three at the three masts. "All friends on deck?" asked Topaz.

"Aye aye, Captain!" the friends called back.

They had sailed just a little way out from

the Green Isle before Jade said, "Come on, girls, we'd better get back." She felt very conscious of the heavy crown on her head. Obsidian was locked up for now, but

she'd find her way out eventually. The sooner they got the Treasure to safety, the better.

The friends gathered in the middle of the ship and held out their hands. "Ring bump!" cried Coral and the five girls touched the stones on their rings together.

Jade had just enough time to shout

"Bye Nes—" before a flash of golden light transported them back to their little dinghy and normal life.

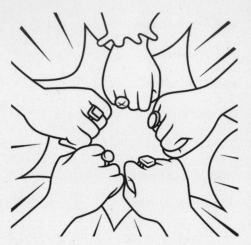

But when they arrived back on Lapis Lake Jade remembered this wasn't normal life – they were in the middle of a race! They were still way out in front.

"Oh!" said Coral. "I forgot we were racing!"

Opal looked at the crown on Jade's head. "Do you want to go and hide the crown now?" she asked.

Jade grinned. "I think we have time to win the race first," she said. "Don't you?"

Topaz pushed a lock of hair away from her eyes. "I was hoping you'd say that! Tighten those

sails!"

Within moments they arrived on the island in the middle of Lapis Lake. To win, they had to find the flag before anyone else did. But the tiny island was covered with trees, bushes and shrubs. The flag was nowhere to be seen.

"Hurry," said Coral, shading her eyes as she looked back out to the lake. "Or the others will catch up!"

Jade looked around and saw the perfect climbing tree, with regularly spaced branches that were not too far apart. From there she would be able to see the whole island! She climbed higher and higher as her friends watched.

"Careful Jade!" shouted Topaz.

"Don't worry about me," Jade called down. "I may be afraid of water, but heights I can handle."

The other competitors were closing in on the island. Jade saw her classmate Eloise jump out of her boat into knee-deep water and start to run for the shore. Hurriedly, Jade scanned the island – there it was – a flash of red among the green and brown.

"There!" she said, pointing her friends in the direction of a scrubby thicket. Topaz reached the thicket first, but Pearl – the smallest – scurried under.

"I've got it!" Pearl said, as she reversed out of the prickly plants and waved the flag in the air.

Jade clambered down the tree and joined her friends. They hugged each other tightly.

"We did it!" they shouted together.

And Jade realised that with her friends by her side they could do anything: win a race, find a gemstone, free their friend, rescue a hundred captured children, stop the evil witch Obsidian.

Easy-peasy.

***

Jade was standing in her green pyjamas beside her bed. She took one last look at the silver crown – her crown, with its bright green gemstone at the front – then put it into her suitcase and pushed it under her bed. *It'll be safe there,* she thought. *So why don't I feel happy?*

The others walked in, dressed in their pyjamas and slippers too. Jade didn't bother to fake a smile for them. They were her best friends, they'd understand if she said she felt down.

But all of them were grinning, Pearl squirming from foot to foot, her mouth clamped shut. Topaz had something behind her back. When they caught sight of the sad look on Jade's face they dropped their smiles and surrounded her. Coral gave her a hug.

"What's the matter?" asked Opal, her eyebrows knotted.

Jade allowed a tear to roll down her cheek.

"Aw guys," she said, her words catching in her throat. "I know I should be happy we saved my island," she sighed. "But ... I'm just so upset about my music box."

The others exchanged a look that Jade didn't quite understand. *Was it pity, or were they ... smiling?*

"I know it was just an object," Jade continued. "But it was the only thing I had from my parents ... and I've lost it forever. I just wish I could hear that song again."

When the tears in Jade's eyes cleared she saw the others weren't looking at her, but at Topaz.

Topaz was grinning. "Which song? This one?"

A tinkly, metallic tune filled the room – a lullaby, both sad and happy at the same time. Jade could hardly believe her ears. Topaz brought the music box out from behind her back. Just like the first time she'd seen it, Jade watched the figures of the parents and their daughter as they walked through the streets.

"Where did you ... how did you ... but I broke it!"

"And we fixed it!" said Topaz, handing Jade the music box.

Opal sat next to Jade and put her arm around her. "You gave it to Topaz in the control room, remember? And we figured it was too precious to throw away."

"So we took it to the school technology department," said Pearl, "and fixed it."

"OK, Mr Davidson helped a little," added

Coral.

"He was very impressed with the mechanism," said Topaz. "Said he'd never seen anything like it."

"We told him it had washed up on the shore," said Pearl.

"He reckoned it would sell for a lot of money," added Coral.

"We told him it was priceless," Opal said finally.

Jade was speechless!

There was a knock at the door and Jade swiped at her face to wipe the tears away. She also kicked her suitcase further under her bed, just in case.

"Girls?" Miss Whitestone peered round the door. "I know you're excited about winning the race," she said, "but it's way too late to be playing music."

"We know, Miss Whitestone."

"Sorry, Miss Whitestone."

"We'll go to bed now, Miss Whitestone."

"No more adventures now," she said. Her voice carried a warning but her smile was kind. "The tide is high and it's much safer to have adventures during the day."

"What does that even mean?" Coral whispered, so only the girls could hear.

"Night night," Miss Whitestone said. And as she closed the door she started whistling ... whistling the tune from Jade's music box!

Jade's mouth dropped open and she looked at the others wide eyed.

"Maybe she heard it through the door," said Topaz, frowning as though she wasn't convinced.

"I wonder what else she heard," said Jade. They had so many secrets. Did Miss Whitestone know some of the truth?

"I don't know," said Opal, climbing into her bed. "My brain hurts. I'm shattered."

"I need my beauty sleep," said Coral, yawning.

"I'm going to dream of rusty staircases tonight," said Pearl.

"And little girls reunited with their favourite bears," said Topaz.

Jade smiled as she pulled the covers up to her chin. She thought about Cindy and her bear, and how happy she'd been to see her parents again. Jade would never see her own mum and dad, but thanks to her princess pirate friends at least she had the music box, and a new family. She smiled and closed her eyes, knowing how happy her parents would be that she'd found them.

TO BE CONTINUED ...

Opal

The Monstrous Forest

Opal can speak with animals, but she will need courage to keep her friends safe in their most dangerous adventure so far!

Can Opal escape the monstrous forest and save the animals and people of the Purple Isle?

Prepare to set sail with the Princess Pirates!

Book 3

ISBN: 978-1-78700-734-5